The Mystery of the
HARD LUCK
RODEO

By Susan Saunders
Illustrated by Melodye Rosales

A STEPPING STONE BOOK

Random House 🏠 New York

To Lamar Hinnant
—S. S.

Text copyright © 1989 by Susan Saunders. Illustrations copyright © 1989 by Melodye Rosales. All rights reserved under International and Pan-American Copyright Conventions. Published in the United States by Random House, Inc., New York, and simultaneously in Canada by Random House of Canada Limited, Toronto.

Library of Congress Cataloging-in-Publication Data:
Saunders, Susan. The mystery of the hard luck rodeo / by Susan Saunders ; illustrated by Melodye Rosales. p. cm.—(A Stepping stone book) SUMMARY: Fourth grader Tommy Price, Jr., and his friend Bonnie Sue, whose families work for area rodeos, investigate the mysterious occurrences that threaten to close down the Red Bluffs rodeo and stop country singer Mel Jones from performing. ISBN: 0-394-82344-3 (pbk.); 0-394-92344-8 (lib. bdg.) [1. Rodeos—Fiction. 2. Mystery and detective stories.] I. Rosales, Melodye, ill. II. Title. PZ7.S2577My 1989 [Fic]—dc19 88-37896

Manufactured in the United States of America 1 2 3 4 5 6 7 8 9 0

Contents

1

The 66th Annual
Red Bluffs Roundup

"We made it!" my dad said as we reached the top of a hill and the whole town of Red Bluffs spread out in front of us. "See that water tower over there?" He pointed through the windshield of his old blue pickup. "The rodeo grounds are right behind it."

I'm Tommy Price, Jr. Most people just call me Junior, although I'm not crazy about the name. Anyway, Junior and Senior were on their way to the Sixty-sixth Annual Red Bluffs Roundup, and my dad's next job.

Maybe you've heard of him—Tommy Price, the bullfighter? A lot of people say he's the best in the business. He's not the kind of bullfighter that wears tight white suits and waves big red capes. He's the kind that dresses up like a clown and saves cowboys when they're thrown by bulls. That's what he'd be doing in Red Bluffs.

As we started down the hill, there was a crash from the back of the truck. My dad stuck his head out the window to yell, "Peppy, quit that!" Peppy's probably the world's meanest Shetland pony, and he'd just given the sideboards the four-hundredth kick since we left home the day before.

"He's hungry," my dad said, making excuses for the little creep because he's part of Daddy's act. But Peppy and I are sworn enemies. Who could like a horse that bites you every chance he gets?

"I'm hungry too, and you don't see me trying to kick the truck apart," I grumbled.

"The Roundup is definitely a good rodeo for eats," Dad said, changing the subject. "The Red Bluffs church ladies sell everything from bar-

becue and potato salad to strawberry cobbler."
He'd already sampled the food, since he'd been
to Red Bluffs a couple of times before. This was
my first trip.

When I was little, my mom and I used to
go everywhere with Daddy, from rodeo to rodeo. Then my little sister Terri came along,
and next Judy. Pretty soon, there wasn't enough
room for all of us in the sleeping trailer. So the
family stuck fairly close to home, and my dad
did a lot of traveling by himself.

This summer, though, as soon as I'd finished fourth grade, he spoke to Mama. "I'm
getting kind of lonesome," he said. "Maybe I'll
take Junior with me."

"I think that's a good idea," my mom said.
"It'll teach him something about the country.
And keep you on your best behavior," she added
with a grin, because my dad has gotten into
some scrapes on his own.

So he and I loaded up Peppy, hitched up
the sleeping trailer, and piled all the clean
clothes we owned into it. We waved good-bye
to Mom and Terri and Judy, and drove west
until we hit Red Bluffs.

"That's the courthouse, and the picture show, and Strebel's, the biggest hardware store in town." My dad pointed out the sights when we stopped at the first red light. "And there's the Tip-Toe Inn . . ."

"Wow! Look at that car!" I exclaimed. Parked at the side of the Tip-Toe Inn was a yellow Cadillac convertible about two blocks long. It had real steer horns on the hood and a four-leaf clover painted on the trunk.

Daddy nodded. "I've seen it before. Belongs to Mel Jones. He's the entertainment for the Roundup."

"That old country singer?"

"That's right—the car's yellow for his biggest hit, 'Yellow Roses on a Blue, Blue Day.' " I was disappointed. I'd been hoping we'd get to hear Alabama, or the Gatlin Brothers, or at least somebody who wasn't ninety years old. I didn't have much time to think about it, though. We'd turned off Main Street to follow the line of big, red rodeo banners leading to the Red Bluffs arena.

A rodeo arena is a huge pen, a rectangle with an announcer's booth perched high over

the bucking chutes at one end, and the roping
chutes and small catch pens at the other end.
In Red Bluffs, big oak trees shade the bleach-
ers on both sides of it. It looks nice and peace-
ful.

My dad and I drove around the arena to
the back of the fairgrounds. A tall fence sepa-
rates the open field that's the contestants'
parking lot from the rest of the grounds.

The guard at the gate hollered, "Good to
see you, Price!" and we rolled right on through.
Daddy squeezed between horse trailers and
campers and trucks to pull up in the shade of
a tree. He'd no sooner stopped the pickup when
he said, "Hey, Junior—isn't that one of your
pals?"

"Bonnie Sue Hood," I murmured.

I hadn't seen Bonnie Sue since last year at
the Atherton Stampede. She didn't look like
she'd changed any. Same frizzy hair, same
brown glasses, same know-it-all, bossy expres-
sion on her round face. And she was still doing
jigsaw puzzles. She had one balanced on her
knees while she was sitting down on the top
step of her parents' Winnebago.

Everybody in Bonnie Sue's family rodeos—
her dad has been World Champion Calf Roper
for years, her mother rides in all the barrel
races, her brother Bud's a bull rider—everybody except Bonnie Sue. Bonnie Sue says she
hates rodeos because they're dirty and smelly
and boring.

"You think I want to spend the rest of my
life hanging out at these things?" she said to
me last year. "No way! I'm going to be a TV
star and make a million dollars!"

"You're going to act?" I said. I mean, Bonnie Sue's not what you'd call good looking.

"Of course not!" Bonnie Sue said huffily. "*Anybody* can act! I'm going to host my own game show. There'll be a huge jigsaw puzzle board with most of the pieces missing. For every piece you fit in right, you get asked a question. For every question you answer, you get . . ." A bull stepped on my dad's foot about then and broke it, so we left the Atherton Stampede before I had to hear about the rest of her game.

Maybe if I was real quiet now. . . . But Peppy kicked the sideboards again. Bonnie Sue looked up, and those brown glasses locked onto me. Dumb horse!

Bonnie Sue jumped up off the top step of the Winnebago and made a beeline for our pickup. She has a mind like a steel trap. I expected her to take up where she'd left off last year: ". . . For every question you answer, you get . . ."

Was I ever surprised when Bonnie Sue leaned through the truck window and hissed, "Boy, is there some weird stuff going on around here!"

2

The Mysterious
Bonnie Sue Hood

Then Bonnie Sue smiled sweetly at my dad. "Hello, Mr. Price," she said in the voice she used for grownups. "It's nice to see you again."

"Hello, Bonnie Sue," he replied. "Nice to see you, too. Junior, I'll unload Peppy—you can visit with your friend."

Thanks a lot, Dad.

Bonnie Sue waited until my father had gotten out of the truck and walked around to the back before she added in a low voice, "It's kind of a puzzle."

"What's a puzzle?" I asked her.

"What's been happening here at the rodeo," Bonnie Sue said. "Come on." She opened the truck door on my side. "I can show you part of it."

"The first piece of the puzzle," Bonnie Sue told me as we walked toward the arena, "is the bucking horses. When we drove up this morning, they were running loose out here in the parking lot."

"You mean they got out of the pen?" I said. Every evening after the rodeo's over, the bucking horses are turned out into the arena so they can stretch their legs and get a good night's rest.

"That's right," Bonnie Sue replied. "It took Mr. Duvall's men over an hour to catch them all."

Mr. Ace Duvall owns the Diamond D Stock Company. He trucks around all the livestock a rodeo might need, like the bucking horses and bulls and the steers for steer wrestling and steer tying. He rents them to one town and then another for their rodeos.

Rodeo livestock are worth a whole lot of

money. For instance, just one good bucking horse costs thousands of dollars. I've heard Mrs. Duvall say Ace cares more about his animals than he does about most people.

"Boy, Mr. Duvall sure must have been mad!" I said to Bonnie Sue.

"Was he ever!" Bonnie Sue answered. "I could hear him hollering all the way over at the Methodist Ladies' Pancake Breakfast. And that's not all—notice anything funny about this program?"

We'd stopped in front of a big bulletin board posted near the arena gate. Bonnie Sue pointed to a copy of the printed program for the first performance.

I read down the list of events and the contestants entered in each one: Bareback Bronc Riding, Calf Roping, Steer Wrestling. Then I got to Entertainment. "Mel Jones" had a smudge in front of it that looked a lot like an *s*.

"*Smel* Jones?" I snorted. "That's pretty funny."

"Mel Jones didn't think so," Bonnie Sue said. "He's really been raising some dust about it."

Somewhere nearby, a man's voice was getting louder and louder. "Sounds like he's not the only one raising dust," I said. "Isn't that Mr. Duvall?"

Bonnie Sue listened for a second. "Yeah, and that's another piece of the puzzle. Mr. Duvall thinks Red Culver let the horses out. I heard him say so to Mrs. Duvall."

"Red wouldn't do that!" I said. Red Culver is one of Mr. Duvall's hired hands. He's one of the nicest guys around.

"The evidence is against him!" Bonnie Sue said darkly.

"Like what?" I asked her.

"For one thing," Bonnie Sue said, "the arena gate standing wide open when only Red and Mr. Duvall have keys to the lock. Mr. Duvall sure didn't open it!"

Bonnie Sue tiptoed up the steps to the announcer's booth. The booth is really just a wooden floor with a roof and one wall. Bonnie Sue crawled across the floor, until she was lying on her stomach with her head poking over the edge. I crawled forward too, until I was even with her.

Raised up about twenty feet in the air like

we were, we had a bird's-eye view of Mr. Duvall and Red Culver. They were standing beside one of the bucking chutes. Red had a hammer in his hand.

Mr. Duvall was dressed the way he always is: with a straw cowboy hat cocked on the left side of his head, a starched Western shirt, and a hand-stitched belt with a silver-and-gold buckle holding up his gray Western pants. A big diamond ring sparkled on the little finger of his left hand.

Red Culver stands about a head taller than Mr. Duvall. He's skinny, with freckles and red curly hair. He was dressed in blue jeans and a denim shirt.

Red just stood there, dead quiet. Mr. Duvall was hopping angrily from one foot to the other in his best lizard boots.

"All thirty-two of my bucking horses, waltzing around the parking lot, trying to break their legs!" Mr. Duvall was shouting. "The padlock on the gate hanging wide open. And you and me with the only keys! Do you have anything to say for yourself?"

"I told you, Ace. I wasn't even here," said Red. "I was buying wood to fix this bucking

chute." He tapped the chute with his hammer.

"So you were careless! You left the key where any joker could pick it up!" fumed Ace Duvall.

"I left the key locked in the big truck," Red said evenly.

"Then how did the gate get open?"

Red shrugged. "I didn't see it. I can't explain it."

"Can you explain what happened at the printers?" said Mr. Duvall through gritted teeth.

"What printers?" Red asked. I thought he looked truly surprised by the question.

"Speedy Printers. It seems a red-headed man dropped by this morning just before they printed the rodeo programs, wanting to take a last look," Mr. Duvall said grimly. "It's just possible that he sneaked that *s* onto the page."

"That doesn't sound good," I muttered to Bonnie Sue. Aside from Red Culver, I couldn't think of a single red-headed man who goes to rodeos.

"Sssh!" Bonnie Sue warned. Mr. Duvall was talking again.

"Where did you buy the lumber for the

bucking chute?" he asked Red. "Strebel's Hardware?"

"That's right," Red said.

"And I guess you didn't notice that Speedy Printers is only two doors away?" Mr. Duvall thundered.

"No, I didn't." Now Red was raising his voice too.

"Well, I think there's one of two things going on here," said Mr. Duvall. "Either we're having a run of awful bad luck, or you're trying to mess up the Diamond D. And since I don't believe in luck . . ."

"You don't have to fire me," Red Culver said. He pitched his hammer down next to Mr. Duvall's right boot. "I quit!"

Red stormed across the arena and out the far gate. Bonnie Sue and I waited until Mr. Duvall snatched up the hammer and marched off in the opposite direction. Then we scrambled to our feet.

"See what I mean?" Bonnie Sue said. "It's a puzzle, all right. Now—if we could just fit some of the pieces together. . . ."

She tore down the stairs and hurried after Mr. Duvall.

3

The Luck of Mr. Jones

Bonnie Sue and I tailed Mr. Duvall around the bucking chutes. He was just about to climb into his truck when a yellow car screeched to a stop beside him, throwing up a cloud of dust.

Mr. Duvall might not have believed in luck, but Mel Jones surely did. Besides the four-leaf clover painted on the trunk of his Cadillac, he had two rabbit's feet hanging from his rear-view mirror. There were horseshoes welded to either side of his license plate, too. When he leaned out of the car on the passenger side, the first thing he said was, "Bad luck! I

have a feeling this rodeo is going to be nothing but bad luck!"

"Mel, we'll fix your name in the next set of programs," Mr. Duvall said wearily.

Mel Jones has a long, flabby face, sad, droopy eyes, and big ears, kind of like a hound's. "It's more than the programs," he replied, tugging on one of his ears.

"Now what's the problem?" Mr. Duvall asked with a sigh.

Mel Jones glanced around warily, as if to make sure no one was listening. Bonnie Sue and I stared hard at the bulletin board on the fence. We pretended we were reading the notices.

Mel Jones lowered his voice to a hoarse whisper. "There was a *hat* on my bed!"

"A hat on your bed," Mr. Duvall repeated slowly.

"At the motel. You know there's nothing unluckier! Isn't that right, George?" Mel asked the man behind the wheel of the Cadillac.

"His driver," Bonnie Sue murmured to me without taking her eyes off the bulletin board. "He also plays the banjo."

"That's right, Mr. Jones," George the driver answered quickly. He was a chunky guy with puffy brown hair.

"Worse than that," Mel Jones went on. "It wasn't *my* hat, or George's either! What I want to know is, whose hat is it? How did it get on *my* bed in *my* motel room?"

He reached into the backseat, felt around with his hand, and came up with a hat. He thrust it out the window at Mr. Duvall.

I'd seen that hat before. It was an old felt one with a crumpled brim. A single gray turkey feather was stuck in the band. It was Red Culver's hat. He always wears it when he's working. Now I remembered that he hadn't had it on when he was standing near the bucking chutes.

If *I* recognized the hat right off, I knew Mr. Duvall would recognize it even sooner. He's seen Red wear it hundreds of times.

But Mr. Duvall didn't give anything away. "I don't think you'll have any more trouble, Mel," he said. Then he took the hat. To Bonnie Sue and me he added, "Excuse me, kids," and climbed into his truck.

"I'd *better* not!" Mel Jones rumbled as the door slammed closed. "Or I'm pulling out of this show, Ace!" He jerked his head back inside the car. "Let's go, George!"

George made a big U-turn near an empty soda stand. Then he roared through the wide outer gate of the contestants' parking lot.

"Well, that's that," Bonnie Sue said, dusting her hands together as though she'd cleared up the whole thing. "Let's get something to eat."

I was starving, so I sure wasn't going to argue with her, at least not until we'd gotten to the Women of the United Churches of Red Bluffs Barbecue. For a dollar seventy-five, I ended up with barbecued ribs, beans, potato salad, corn bread, and iced tea. Bonnie Sue had already eaten lunch, so she just picked out a piece of cherry pie with vanilla ice cream on top.

Once we were sitting at one of the long tables, I said, "What did you mean, 'that's that'?"

"The bucking horses turned loose with Red's key. 'Smel' Jones after a red-headed man showed up at the printers. Red's hat on the bed. What does it add up to?" She answered herself smartly, "Red Culver did it all." Bonnie Sue took a satisfied bite of pie. "All the pieces fit together."

"But why would Red want to do those things?" I asked her.

Bonnie Sue shrugged her shoulders and sniffed. "Maybe he wanted a raise from Mr. Duvall, and Mr. Duvall wouldn't give him one." Mr. Duvall is known for being cheap. "Or maybe he was ready to take a vacation, and Mr. Duvall said no." She shrugged again. Then she waved her fork in my face. "You can fit puzzles together in two ways, Junior," she said. "By shapes or by colors. In this puzzle, the color is *Red*."

Somehow, I couldn't believe it.

4

Bonnie Sue's
853rd Grand Entry

After we finished eating, Bonnie Sue went back
to working on her latest jigsaw puzzle. I hung
around the sleeping trailer, watching my dad
get ready for the eight o'clock show.

First he pulled on his bright-red tights, and
over those some cutoff Levis with a square
striped patch on the rear and a bandanna
hanging out of the back pocket. Then he but-
toned up his white shirt with the big red hearts.
Socks and blue sneakers went on his feet.

He sat down in front of the round mirror

and started dabbing on his clown makeup: white circles around his eyes and mouth, outlined with black paint. Then he filled in the rest of his face with red paint. He added a few black freckles here and there, and colored one tooth black right in the front of his mouth. The last thing he did was pull on an orange wig to cover up his own brown hair.

"What do you think, Junior?" he asked me when he'd finished.

"Looking good, Dad," I said.

"Won't be long before I'll have you out in the arena with me," he said with a grin.

"Not me," I told him. My dad's been bruised, broken, cut, stitched, stepped on, tossed in the air, and run over by bulls. I think he's great, but I also think you have to be a little crazy to mess around with two-thousand-pound animals with horns. "I believe I'll stay in the stands."

"Well, let's see what kind of mood old Peppy's in," Daddy said. He pulled an apple out of our cooler, and both of us climbed down from the trailer. Daddy grabbed Peppy's bridle out of the back of our truck.

My dad had made a little pen of wooden stakes and rope at one side of the oak tree we'd parked under. Peppy was standing in a corner of the pen, chomping on some hay. As soon as he saw us, he kind of edged himself around until his back end was toward us.

"He'd like nothing better than to get in a good swift kick!" I said.

"Aw, he's not so bad," Daddy said. He talked softly to Peppy until he got him to turn around, and gave him a couple of bites of the apple. Dad stuffed the rest of it in a pocket of his cut-offs and slipped the bridle over Peppy's head.

"You come on back here when the steer wrestling starts, Junior. Bring him and the blanket to the arena gate, okay?" The blanket is part of their act.

"Sure, Dad," I said.

He slipped the ropes off a couple of the wooden stakes. Then he stuck one red leg over Peppy's bare back—the horse won't put up with a saddle—and kind of eased onto him.

"Here we go, Pep!" Dad said, guiding Peppy around the trucks and trailers. Peppy's one of the shorter Shetlands. So when my dad's sitting on him, the bottoms of Dad's sneakers are only about six inches off the ground. "Got to line up." He rode away, his legs dangling.

I grabbed myself a seat in the grandstand closest to the main arena gate. I was just in time to hear the rodeo announcer say, "Good evening, rodeo fans—welcome to the Sixty-sixth performance of the Red Bluffs Rodeo. And now for the excitement and color of the Grand Entry!"

All rodeos start with the Grand Entry, a long parade of contestants on horses loping around the arena in time to marching music. I was busy watching for my dad and Peppy, so I didn't notice Bonnie Sue Hood until she practically sat on me.

"Scoot over," she ordered over the music. "Let me squeeze in." The grandstand was pretty filled up by then. Bonnie Sue sighed real loud. "I figured out I've seen at least eight-hundred-fifty-two Grand Entries in my life, all just alike. There's your dad. Hiii, Mr. Price!" Bonnie Sue screeched.

Daddy and Peppy were bouncing along in front of Kyle Johnson on his mule, Sal. Kyle was the other clown at the Red Bluffs Roundup.

Usually there are at least two clowns at every rodeo. One is a bullfighter, like my dad. Bull-fighters jump right in front of a charging bull, or grab hold of his tail, or pat his head while he's trying to run over them. Their job is to keep the bull rider safe once he's on the ground by leading the bull away from him.

The second clown is a barrel man. Barrel men get the bull's attention. Then they jump into a barrel to get out of his way. Kyle Johnson is a barrel man. He's heavier than Daddy, and older, and he can't move quite as fast.

"Why are you out here in the dust and dirt, watching this boring rodeo?" I said to Bonnie Sue.

"Somebody has to keep an eye on things, Junior," she said importantly.

5

Junior's Bad Luck

After the Grand Entry, my dad took Peppy back to his pen. Then he helped out in the rodeo arena for the first part of the show. I was stuck with Bonnie Sue Hood through the bareback bronc riding, the saddle broncs, and the calf roping. Ace Duvall was running around in the arena, shouting orders and moving the show along. Finally, it was time for the steer wrestling to start. That meant I had to go get Peppy again.

I climbed into the trailer first to pick up

the blue blanket and an apple bribe. When I stepped outside, I saw Mel Jones's yellow Cadillac parked one car over.

Mel was standing next to it in a glittery white suit, listening to George the driver.

"Don't forget the hat on the bed, Mr. Jones," George was saying. "Very bad luck. Maybe you'd better not take a chance tonight. It might be safer if you canceled."

"Ace was sure there wouldn't be any more trouble," Mel rumbled. "Besides, what would the crowd do for entertainment?"

"I could play 'em a couple of tunes on the banjo," George said. "I've got some new stuff. Of course," he added quickly, "they wouldn't be nearly as happy with me as they would with you."

"You bet they wouldn't!" When Mel Jones laughs, it sounds sort of like he's barking.

"I'd do my best," said George, sounding peevish.

"But you're not Mel Jones, are you?" Mel Jones said.

George didn't answer that.

Then Peppy stamped his feet a few times and snorted at me, so I didn't get to hear the end of it. I stuck the apple in his mouth to keep his teeth busy. Then I grabbed the bridle and led him over to the arena.

As many times as I'd seen my dad and Peppy do their act, I still thought it was funny. Daddy played an old goldminer, and Peppy was his faithful packhorse. Daddy walked around pretending to chip at rocks with a hammer while Peppy stole things out of his pockets—first his bandanna, next the apple.

Then came the best part. All the lights in the arena went off except for the two nearest Dad and Peppy. Dad lay down on the ground, and Peppy lay down beside him. Dad carefully arranged the blue blanket over himself. In a second, Peppy reached out and pulled the blanket off Dad with his teeth. Lots of laughs from the crowd.

Then Daddy spread the blanket over both of them. Everything was quiet for a moment, except for my dad snoring loudly. Suddenly Peppy rolled all the way over in the other direction, leaving Dad without a blanket at all. The horse wrapped himself up in it completely!

In the middle of all the applause at the end of the act, Bonnie Sue jabbed me with a bony elbow.

"Ouch!" I said, rubbing my ribs. "What is it?"

"Red Culver's back!" she hissed.

"Where?! Are you sure?" I asked her.

"Behind the chutes!" Bonnie Sue answered. "Who else has red hair? Don't turn around!" she warned, jabbing me again. "He might see you looking for him."

"What do you think he's doing here?" I stared straight ahead as a man on a tractor smoothed out the sand in the arena for the ladies' barrel race.

"Making trouble," Bonnie Sue said grimly. "Maybe he's going to let out the bucking horses again." They were in a pen behind the chutes, not far from where we were sitting.

Daddy walked through the arena gate with Peppy just then. "Junior, I'll take him back to the truck," my dad called out. "I want to wrap my knee before the bull riding." Sometimes Dad wears an Ace bandage on his right knee, the one a bull rammed in Tuba City last year.

"Okay, Dad!" I called back. "Do you see him now?" I whispered to Bonnie Sue.

She cut her eyes over toward the dark behind the bucking chutes. "No, but I'll bet he's still there," she replied. "I guess we should tell Mr. Duvall."

I shook my head. "We ought to figure out what Red's up to first. I wish there was some way to get closer to him without him noticing us."

That's when I spotted a barrel in the shadows outside the arena gate. In the ladies' barrel race, the contestants run their horses in a pattern around three barrels. The three that would be used were already inside the arena, so the barrel lying on its side outside the gate had to be an extra.

"I'm going to try to slip inside that barrel," I said to Bonnie Sue.

"Great idea!" Bonnie Sue said. "Wait until

everybody's watching the barrel racers."

"Our first little lady tonight is Debbie Hall, from Calverton, Oklahoma!" the announcer called.

As Debbie went steaming through the arena gate on her dun horse, headed for the first barrel, I strolled toward *my* barrel as though I didn't have a care in the world. As soon as I figured all eyes were on the racer, I scrambled into one end of the barrel on the ground.

Now I was facing the pen full of bucking horses, but it was dark back there. I couldn't

pick anything out that wasn't a light-colored horse or a fence post. I decided that I'd lie still, keeping my eyes peeled, and wait for Red to give himself away by moving. Where was he, anyway?

Barrel racers were whizzing past my barrel every thirty seconds or so. But I was trying so hard to spot Red that I didn't pay any attention to what was going on in the arena behind me.

It wasn't until I heard somebody yell, "I'll roll this one in, Kyle!" that I took notice. But by then it was too late.

Suddenly my barrel spun around. Then it rolled over and over and over again, until I felt as though I'd gotten caught in a washing machine.

What I'd gotten caught in was a lot worse than that.

"Ladies and gentlemen," I heard the announcer call, "here's the event you've all been waiting for! It's time for the most dangerous contest between man and beast at any rodeo: the death-defying wild Brahma bull riding!"

And there I was in my barrel, inside the arena, right in the line of fire!

6
Tommy Price, Jr.– Barrel Man

"Turn your attention to chute three, folks," the announcer said. "It's gonna be Robby Burke on . . . Tornado!"

My barrel was aimed straight at chute three. Even if I'd wanted one, I couldn't have had a better view of Robby Burke nodding that he was ready. The wide white gate with a 3 on it swung open, and Tornado exploded out of it with Robby on his back.

I scrunched down in the very bottom of the barrel, trying to make myself as small as I could. And I held my breath. All I could hope was that Bonnie Sue Hood was telling somebody where I was.

Tornado was a giant spotted bull with crooked horns and a big hump. Robby Burke was squeezed up tight against the hump. He was hanging on to the bull rope tied around the animal's middle with one hand. His other hand waved in the breeze above his head.

I could see my dad over to the right, watching, watching, ready to make his move if Robby Burke got thrown off.

A couple of hops out of the chute, and Tornado jumped high into the air. He came down stiff-legged, on all four hooves, with such a *whump!* that I thought for sure Robby's head would snap off his neck. Robby barely had time to steady himself when Tornado lived up to his name and started spinning to the left. He spun until I had to close my eyes, feeling seasick. I couldn't begin to imagine how Robby Burke felt!

After what seemed like hours, there was a *beep!* over the loudspeaker.

"There's the buzzer, folks," said the announcer. "Robby stayed on the required eight seconds. And it was quite a ride! Let's give him a big round of applause . . . Uh-oh. He's having some trouble getting loose," the announcer added. "Looks like his hand's caught in the bull rope."

Tornado was only about twenty feet away from my barrel, so I could see it all. Even though Robby Burke was no longer straddling the bull, he was still tied to him. He was dangling from the rope at a point just behind the bull's hump—and he couldn't get his hand loose! Tornado had his big ugly head turned. He was trying to hook Robby with one of those crooked horns!

That's when my dad raced over. He danced around Tornado's head, slapping the bull on the nose. He cut it so close that one of Tornado's horns missed the seat of his pants by only a few inches.

Then Kyle Johnson showed up too, from somewhere behind me. "Yooo-hoooo!" Kyle yelled. "Tornadooo!" And he pawed up some dirt with his feet to get the bull's attention.

While Daddy and Kyle kept Tornado busy,

Robby Burke yanked on the bull rope again and again with his free hand. Finally, as Tornado started pawing the dirt himself, Robby jerked his hand loose. He just stood there for a second, wobbling a little.

Tornado swung his head around. Before he could make up his mind to do anything about Robby, though, Kyle waved a red bandanna in his direction. Kyle also bellowed as loud as he could.

Tornado whirled toward Kyle and lowered his head. That gave Daddy a chance to rush in, grab Robby by the arm, and push him toward the fence.

"Watch him. He's gonna charge you, Kyle!" Daddy shouted over his shoulder.

"I've got a barrel right here!" Kyle shouted back. "Here he comes . . ." Kyle added to himself in a lower voice.

Suddenly my barrel was turned on its end, and a pair of track shoes came down on my head!

"I'm in here already!" I hollered.

"Junior!" Kyle hopped out of the barrel and stood behind it. "Brace yourself, boy," he warned. "He's headin' this way!"

Kyle must have jumped sideways when Tornado charged. By that time I was down in the bottom of the barrel, so I couldn't see anything. But I could sure *feel* it! WHAM! Tornado hit the barrel going about ninety miles an hour!

Rodeo barrels are made of hard, thick rubber. Tornado bounced mine around like a kid kicking a can. We flipped head over heels a couple of times, that barrel and I.

"Are you okay, Junior?" Kyle shouted when we finally came to rest on our sides.

"Yeah—I g-guess so," I answered as loud as I could. I was so scared that my teeth were chattering!

"Junior?!" my dad roared.

"He's *in the barrel*!" Kyle yelled.

Bam! Tornado hit my barrel again. The barrel was already lying on its side this time, so it just rolled.

"Hey, ugly!" I heard later that Daddy grabbed the bull's tail then and stuck to it like a burr. Tornado forgot all about the barrel, trying to shake my dad loose.

Meanwhile, Bonnie Sue had run to the announcer's booth. He called for help. Kyle pushed the barrel against the fence and turned it right-side up again. Mr. Ace Duvall himself helped me over the top.

"How about that, folks?" the rodeo announcer said. "They start bull fighting early in the Price family! Let's give Tommy Junior a big hand!"

I didn't hear much of it, because my ears were ringing something awful. When I tried to walk, my knees gave out. But everything else seemed to be working. Mostly I was worried about the big hand I was going to get from Daddy, right where I sit down!

7
More Clues

Ace helped me over to our trailer and made me lie down. I was beat, but I was too worried about what my dad was going to say to fall asleep.

Daddy showed up at the end of the first half of the bull riding. "I guess you're too big to spank, Junior," he said sternly. Then he gave me a hug. "I'm just glad you're okay. If anything happened to you, your mama would come after both of us."

Daddy left to get ready for the second half

of the bull riding, which came right after "Smel" Jones's entertainment. I tried to stay awake, but my eyes closed before Mr. Jones had even plucked the first note on his guitar.

When I opened the trailer door early the next morning, Bonnie Sue Hood was there, waiting for me.

"Finally!" she said snippily. Then she added a little more politely, "How're you feeling, Junior?"

"My head's kind of sore, and I've got bruises in more places than I knew I *had* places," I told her. "Otherwise, okay."

"Did you *ever* miss something last night!" Bonnie Sue said.

"Like what?" I didn't think she could come up with anything to equal a game of kick-the-can with Tornado.

"More bad luck for Mel Jones," she answered.

"What happened?"

Bonnie Sue told me how Ace's men had dragged a wooden stage into the arena with the tractor. Mel Jones rode out to it on a dapple-gray horse, his white suit shining in the lights.

George had to walk alongside him, carrying Mel's guitar and his own banjo.

Both men climbed onstage. Mel strummed a couple of chords. Then he stepped up to the microphone. He'd just started to tell the crowd how special his guitar was . . . when he fell right through the floor!

"You're kidding!" I said.

"Nope! He was sticking out of the stage from his waist up, hollering his head off!" Bonnie Sue replied.

"What happened then?"

"George tried to pull him out"—she started to giggle—"and he lost his wig!"

"Mel?" I asked.

"No—George!" said Bonnie Sue. "He's bald as an egg under that puffy brown hair. Anyway, some of Mr. Duvall's men hoisted Mel Jones out of the hole. Mel and George and Ace had a big powwow out there in the arena. I think George said he'd play in Mel's place, because he kind of waved his banjo at Ace. But then Mel must have said he'd go on. Because he ended up singing after all."

"Did the boards in the stage break, or were

they rotten, or what?" I asked her.

"That's why I'm here so early," Bonnie Sue said. "I think we ought to take a look at the stage before they fix it. Don't forget, Red Culver's still hanging around," she added. As if she needed to remind me. What was I doing in the barrel the night before, if not trying to spy on Red?!

Then my dad opened the trailer door. "I thought I heard somebody talking out here. What are the two of you up to?"

"Oh, we thought we'd go for a walk, Mr. Price," Bonnie Sue said breezily.

"Good. I'm counting on you to keep Junior out of trouble, Bonnie Sue."

We stopped off at the Hoods' Winnebago. Bonnie Sue slipped inside for a flashlight. Then we hurried over to the arena.

They'd dragged the stage out through the gate, but not much farther. Nobody was around yet, so we climbed up on top of it. The hole was about as big as Mel Jones is wide. The edges were jagged.

"It looks like the boards just broke," I said to Bonnie Sue. "Maybe Mr. Jones ought to go on a diet."

"I want to check it out underneath," Bonnie Sue told me.

As sore as I was, I couldn't let her do it alone. What if she actually found something? So both of us lowered ourselves through the hole. We squatted down under the stage, and Bonnie Sue turned on her flashlight.

"Mmm-hmm," she said as soon as the beam lit the edge of the hole from underneath.

"Wow!" I exclaimed. I touched one of the boards. "Under here, the edges are completely smooth. Somebody sawed these boards halfway through . . ."

". . . and let Mel Jones break them the rest of the way," said Bonnie Sue. "Hey!" She moved the flashlight beam over an inch. "What's this?"

She pulled something off the point of a nail. Then she stuck it under my nose. It was one . . . short . . . red . . . hair!

8

One Red Hair

While we were waiting in line for pancakes at the Methodist Ladies' tent, I looked more closely at the hair Bonnie Sue had found. "It's thicker than Red's, and it's not the right color. Besides, this hair is straight," I pointed out, handing it back to her. "Red's is curly."

"Maybe it straightened out hanging on that nail," Bonnie Sue argued. She stuck the hair in her shirt pocket. "And can you name one other red-headed man who rodeos?"

"Are you talking about Red Culver?" a

cowboy standing in line behind us asked.

"Yes," Bonnie Sue said.

"I just heard that Ace Duvall had him arrested last night," the cowboy said. "For malicious mischief."

Whatever that meant, it didn't sound good for Red.

"I have a feeling the bad luck around this rodeo is going to stop," Bonnie Sue announced. "As long as you stay out of barrels, Junior," she added with a giggle.

But I thought a lot about that short, red hair that day. There was something funny about it that I couldn't quite put my finger on . . . until late that afternoon, while my dad was getting ready for the evening show.

He'd dressed in his clown clothes and painted on all of his makeup. The last thing he did was pull on his wig.

It hit me all of a sudden. That's what was strange about the hair Bonnie Sue had found. It didn't look like real hair. It was too thick, too stiff . . . too *nylon!*

I jumped up and threw open the door of the trailer.

"Where are you going in such a hurry?" my dad wanted to know.

"Over to Bonnie Sue's for a second," I said.

When I knocked on the door of the Winnebago, Bonnie Sue answered it.

"The red hair," I said. "Can I see it?"

Bonnie Sue shook her head. "Red's in jail already, so there wasn't any point in keeping it. I threw it out. What's the problem?" she added when she saw me frown.

"I think it was a hair from a red *wig,*" I told her. "It looked a lot like the hair in Daddy's orange wig. You know, thick, stiff, made of nylon or something."

"A wig!" Bonnie Sue closed the door behind her and sat down hard on the top step of the Winnebago. "And I threw out the evidence!"

"Where did you throw it?" I asked her.

"Somewhere between here and the Methodist Ladies' tent," she replied gloomily. "About a mile's worth of places to look, and the sun's setting."

I sat down on the bottom step and sighed. "Well, at least if anything else goes wrong, we'll know Red didn't do it."

I'd barely closed my mouth when Bonnie Sue's brother, Bud, came swaggering along. Bull riders all have a kind of roll to their walk, and after last night I could understand why.

"Hey, squirts!" Bud said. "Either of you seen a guitar?"

"What's that supposed to mean?" Bonnie Sue said.

"Somebody stole ol' Smel's guitar out of the Cadillac a while ago," Bud said. "He's going bananas."

9

The Disappearing Guitar

Bonnie Sue and I found Mr. Jones near the announcer's booth. And Bud wasn't fooling. Mel was going *crazy!*

"The worst luck I've ever had in my life! Almost killed myself falling through a stage, and this is the last straw!" he was howling. "That guitar is my lucky piece. I've been playing on it since I was a baby, and it belonged to my granddaddy before that!" He turned to Mr. Duvall, who was part of a growing crowd, and stamped his big foot. "I'll sue you, Ace! And I'll sue the Red Bluffs Rodeo Association, and the mayor, and . . . and . . ."

Mr. Duvall held up the hand with the diamond on it for silence. "Give us a chance to look for it first, Mel," he said. "We know it disappeared in the last hour and a half, since you drove into the fairgrounds. We're all fenced off back here, and nobody's driven out of the contestants' gate. The guard's sure of that. There's a good possibility the guitar's still around."

"Even if you *do* find it, I'm not singing tonight!" Mel Jones was revving up again. "I'm getting as far away from this place as I can. As fast as I can!" He stomped toward the yellow Cadillac, which was parked near the soda stand.

Ace shook his head. "I guess we'll have to cancel the entertainment," he said to Mrs. Duvall.

"And this time we even spelled his name right," she said sadly.

They'd started up the stairs of the announcer's booth when George the driver grabbed Ace's arm.

"Mr. Duvall, I'll go on for him," George said. "I sing pretty good. I know all of his songs. And I've written a few myself."

"We just might have to call on you, George," said Mr. Duvall. "But first we'd better look for that guitar."

"Thanks, Mr. Duvall," George said with a big smile.

"At least somebody's happy," said Bonnie Sue as the crowd broke up.

"Somebody sure is," I said. I watched George as he strolled toward the yellow Cadillac. "He's used to wearing a wig, too."

"George the driver?" Bonnie Sue wrinkled her forehead.

"And banjo picker. And songwriter. And singer," I said. "I think George wants to be a star."

"You may be right, Junior," Bonnie Sue said slowly. "We'd better keep an eye on him."

Mr. Duvall got together a bunch of workers and cowboys, and they looked everywhere, from the trunks of the cars in the contestants' parking lot to the stalls in the horse barn. George joined in the hunt too. But Mel's guitar didn't show up.

"It's almost time for the Grand Entry," Ace said at last. "But after the show, we're going to search every inch of the fairgrounds, and every car coming in and going out."

George took his banjo and a suitcase out of the Cadillac. Mel Jones roared away without a parting word.

Bonnie Sue and I watched George through the Grand Entry, the bareback bronc riding, the calf roping, and the saddle broncs. He sat in the stands, cool as a cucumber. When the steer wrestling was about to start, I had to go get Peppy.

"Take your time," Bonnie Sue said with a yawn. "He's not moving anyway."

Peppy was in one of his nastier moods that night. He folded back his ears and showed his teeth as soon as he saw me. Even after I'd bribed him with an apple, he whirled away from me every time I reached for his bridle.

I hunkered down beside the truck, hoping he'd get hold of himself. And that's when I heard the noise. It was quiet where we were parked. You could hear the announcer over the loudspeaker, but it was far enough away to sound more like a buzz. The applause was like a friendly murmur. The noises I was hearing were much closer, sharp little tapping sounds. Then there was a thud, and a noise like cloth ripping.

I stood up very carefully and peered into the darkness. I couldn't really see much, but I decided that the noises were coming from outside the Hoods' Winnebago! Was somebody trying to break in?

Suddenly I saw a dark shape slide out from *under* the Winnebago. The shape lay still for a moment. Then it stood up. Lights from a faraway car flashed across it and disappeared, but not before I'd gotten a better look.

The larger shape was holding a smaller shape. What I was seeing was definitely a man— a man carrying a guitar!

Mel Jones's guitar had been hidden right under our noses, or at least Bonnie Sue's—underneath the Hoods' Winnebago!

The man moved away from me. Then I heard two or three cowboys walking in our direction, talking and laughing. The man heard them too. He swung around and glided toward our truck. I crouched down again as fast as I could. The man came closer. And closer. I could hear him breathing. He changed direction a little, and fell straight over Peppy's rope fence!

The man grunted when he hit the ground. His legs got caught in the rope. He started kicking, but he couldn't pull them loose while he was still holding on to the guitar.

Peppy was on top of him in a second, snort-

ing and squealing like a wild stallion. I didn't want the man to be hurt, or Mel Jones's guitar, either. I grabbed Peppy's blue blanket, which was lying over the side of the truck, and scooted under the ropes. I threw the blanket over Peppy's head. And suddenly the truck lights went on, practically blinding me.

"Are you okay, Junior? " Bonnie Sue Hood called out.

"You bet!" I said, hanging on to Peppy and staring straight down at George the driver.

Two seconds later Daddy turned up, looking for Peppy and me. Next came Ace Duvall, and finally the Red Bluffs Sheriff's Department, red lights flashing.

At first George said he had found the guitar hidden in a tree on the fairgrounds. But when I told about him crawling under the Winnebago for it, he clammed up. He didn't start talking again until the sheriff pried open his suitcase. Inside it, laid out on top of George's clothes, was a bright red wig.

Then you couldn't shut George up. Yes, he'd stolen the key to the arena by opening the locked door of the truck with a coat hanger. That's when he'd borrowed Red Culver's hat, too. Yes, he'd changed "Mel" to "Smel" at Speedy Printers and sawed through the boards of the stage. When Peppy took after him, George was planning on burning Mel's guitar to cinders.

"I'm better than Mel is. I just needed a chance," George whined. "I figured I'd make the Red Bluffs Roundup look like bad luck so

Mel would pull out. What could be worse luck than having his granddaddy's guitar disappear—permanently?"

"Poor Red had the bad luck, just because the wig matched his hair," Ace Duvall said then. "I think I'll have to give that a boy a raise."

"Do you think George is any good?" I said to Bonnie Sue as the sheriff nudged George into a police car.

Bonnie Sue shrugged her shoulders. "He'll have plenty of time to practice where he's going, that's for sure."

"I understand Mel Jones put up a hundred-dollar reward for that guitar," Daddy told us. "The two of you'll split it, of course. Fifty dollars will still buy you a lot of jigsaw puzzles, Bonnie Sue."

"Yes, sir," she replied. "But I think I'm giving that up."

"No game show?" I asked her.

"I think I'm going into the detective business," Bonnie Sue said. Then she cut her eyes over to me. "Junior, I'll be needing a partner. . . ."

About the Author

SUSAN SAUNDERS really knows about rodeos. She started going to them with her parents when she was just a baby—her father was a professional calf roper. She also competed in youth rodeos as a barrel racer and a breakaway calf roper until she was about 18. "I've probably seen as many Grand Entries," she says, "as Bonnie Sue Hood.

"The first rodeos were contests between cowboys on neighboring ranches," she adds. "The towns of Pecos, Texas, and Prescott, Arizona, both claim to be the site, about a hundred years ago, of the first public rodeo, with trophies for the winners."

Susan Saunders grew up in Texas and now lives in New York.

About the Illustrator

MELODYE ROSALES enjoys illustrating books for young readers because, she says, "Having two children of my own has really opened up this whole new wonderful world for me. I loved illustrating *The Mystery of the Hard Luck Rodeo* because it's funny and full of adventure. And I learned a lot about rodeos, too."

Melodye Rosales lives in Chicago with her husband and their two children.

Washington County Library System

HEADQUARTERS
WILLIAM ALEXANDER PERCY MEMORIAL LIBRARY
841 MAIN STREET
GREENVILLE, MISSISSIPPI 38701